KU-622-335

HERCULES

BENJAMIN HULME-CROSS

Illustrated by
Alessia Trunfio

BLOOMSBURY EDUCATION
LONDON OXFORD NEW YORK NEW DELHI SYDNEY

Guide to names

This guide will help you read and say some of the names in these stories.

Hercules	Herk-you-lees
Cerberus	Ser-ber-russ
Hesperides	Hess-per-i-dees
Zeus	Zooss
Charon	Kair-on
Hades	Hay-dees

X079590

HERCULES

Bloomsbury Education
Bloomsbury Publishing Plc
50 Bedford Square, London, WC1B 3DP, UK

BLOOMSBURY, BLOOMSBURY EDUCATION and the Diana logo
are trademarks of Bloomsbury Publishing Plc

First published in 2020 by Bloomsbury Publishing Plc

Text copyright © Benjamin Hulme-Cross
Illustrations copyright © Alessia Trunfio

Benjamin Hulme-Cross and Alessia Trunfio have asserted their rights under the Copyright, Designs and Patents Act, 1988, to be identified as Author and Illustrator of this work

All rights reserved. No part of this publication may be reproduced or transmitted in any form or by any means, electronic or mechanical, including photocopying, recording, or any information storage or retrieval system, without prior permission in writing from the publishers

A catalogue record for this book is available from the British Library

ISBN: PB: 978-1-4729-7109-8
ePDF: 978-1-4729-7110-4 ePUB: 978-1-4729-7112-8

2 4 6 8 10 9 7 5 3 1

Typeset by Integra Software Services Pvt. Ltd.

Printed and bound in China by Leo Paper Press, Heshan Guangdong

All papers used by Bloomsbury Publishing Plc are natural, recyclable products from wood grown in well managed forests and other sources. The manufacturing processes conform to the environmental regulations of the country of origin

Catch Up is a charity which aims to address the problem of underachievement that has its roots in literacy and numeracy difficulties.

To find out more about our authors and books visit www.bloomsbury.com and sign up for our newsletters

CONTENTS

The Lion's Mane

Hercules was a Greek hero. He was very big. He was very strong. And he liked to show off.

One day a goddess spoke to Hercules. She asked him to choose what kind of life he would like.

"I can grant you an easy, happy life," said the goddess. "You won't have to do any hard work. You will always have enough food. And you will have lots of fun."

Hercules thought that kind of life sounded great. But then the goddess spoke again.

"Or, I can grant you a hard life," she said. "You will have to fight. You will have to suffer. But you will be famous forever."

Hercules thought that kind of life sounded even better.

“I want to be famous forever,” he said.

“Then go to the king and ask him what he wants you to do,” she said.

So, Hercules went to see the king. The king did not like the look of Hercules.

“Who are you?” he asked.

“I am the great Hercules!” said Hercules. “I am going to be famous forever!”

The king was angry. He thought Hercules was a show-off.

“Prove it!” said the king. “In Nemea there is a lion. It has been killing people for years. Every hunter who goes after it gets eaten. If you’re so great, kill that lion, and make sure you bring me the skin. I’m not going to be tricked by a great hulk like you!”

Hercules picked up his club and set off for Nemea. On his back were his bow and arrows and in his belt was his bronze knife.

When he got to Nemea, he asked people about the lion.

“People say it is huge!” said an old woman.

"People say it is terrible!" said an old man.

"It keeps eating people!" said a young boy who was sitting by a river. "I've seen it."

Hercules sat down next to the boy and asked him what he knew about the lion.

"The lion has claws like swords," said the boy. "It has teeth like spears. People have been hunting it for five years, and none of them ever came back. If you go up that mountain you can see their bones near the lion's cave!

"But you won't see their skulls. The lion likes crunching on the skulls."

Then the boy stopped talking. He was looking at the beautiful bronze knife Hercules had in his belt.

"Are you thinking I will be able to kill the lion with this knife?" asked Hercules.

"Um..." said the boy and he shook his head. "I was thinking, if you are going off to get eaten by the lion, can I have your knife?"

Hercules was cross.

"How dare you?" he said. "I am Hercules and I will be famous forever! How can you think that I will be eaten by a lion?"

Then Hercules set off up the mountain.

Hercules was very strong and he was very big, and he was not afraid of anything. But the trouble with being so big and strong was that it made walking up mountains very hard work.

The hot sun beat down on his neck. The sweat poured down his face. He really needed a drink of water.

Hercules couldn't see a cave. He couldn't see any bones. He began to think the boy might have been tricking him.

"Stupid boy," Hercules thought. "He could have told me to bring some water."

He looked back down the mountain. Far below, he could see the river. This made Hercules want a drink even more.

Just then something hit his shoulder.

"Ow!" shouted Hercules. He saw a small stone rolling away down the mountain. Hercules looked up.

He saw a girl sitting on a rock not far away. She had another stone in her hand.

"You little—" Hercules yelled. The girl just laughed and ran off up the mountain. Hercules ran after her but he could not keep up. She jumped from rock to rock like a mountain goat and then disappeared behind a huge rock.

Hercules heard shouting. Soon a man appeared. He was pulling the girl along by the hand.

"I am sorry, sir," said the man. "My daughter is a pest. Like a flea!" The girl laughed and pulled her hand free. She ran back behind the rock.

"Would you like some water?" said the man.

"Yes please!" said Hercules.

The man brought him some water and Hercules drank it quickly.

"I suppose you are looking for the lion?" the man asked.

"Yes, I am," said Hercules.

"You must be mad!" said the man. "I'm sure you've heard the stories about the lion."

"Yes, yes!" said Hercules. "Claws like swords. Teeth like spears. Bones everywhere. No skulls."

"Can I have your bow and arrows when the lion has finished with you?" asked the man.

“No you can’t!” said Hercules crossly. “Tell me what you know about the lion.”

“I can tell you four things,” said the old man. “The lion’s cave is up the mountain. The cave has two entrances so the lion can’t be trapped. The lion’s skin is so tough it can’t be hurt by arrows. And the lion likes to come out of its cave in the early evening.”

“Thank you,” said Hercules. “You have been very helpful, but your daughter is a pest!”

Hercules set off again up the mountain. Far above him he could see the two cave entrances that the man had told him about.

Hercules was very tired. His feet hurt, his back hurt and his legs hurt. He looked down. The rocks he was stepping on were white and they made a crunching sound as he walked. Hercules stopped and looked at the rocks more closely. He felt sick. It wasn't rock that he was walking on now. It was a pile of human bones, but there were no skulls with the bones. Big, strong Hercules was afraid.

He walked on over the bones as quietly as he could. He found a rock to hide behind, near the cave entrance, and sat down to wait for evening. Soon he was fast asleep.

Hercules woke just as the sun was setting over the hills. He rubbed his tired legs and peeped out from behind the rock to watch the cave entrances.

And there it was!

The lion really was huge! It was much bigger than any living thing Hercules had ever seen. Its skin shone like bronze in the evening sun. It lifted up one of its paws and licked its claws. They really were like swords.

"The goddess said it wouldn't be an easy life," thought Hercules.

He put an arrow in his bow and pulled back the string.

His bow was strong enough to sink an arrow in a thick pine tree. Surely it would kill the lion.

Hercules aimed the arrow at the lion's heart. Just then, the lion yawned. Its teeth really were like spears.

Hercules shot the arrow. It flew through the air. His aim was perfect. The arrow struck the lion in just the right place, but... the arrow fell to the ground.

The lion gave a loud roar. It was not hurt but it was very angry. Then it sprang into the nearest cave entrance.

Hercules didn't know what to do. If he followed the lion into the cave it might attack him. That would be good because he could fight it. Or it might just run out of the other cave entrance and disappear. Hercules had to find some way of blocking one of the cave entrances.

Next to one of the entrances was a big rock. Hercules ran over to it. He pushed the rock as hard as he could. No normal man could have done it, but Hercules was no normal man. He was very big and very strong. Slowly, the rock began to move. Then it began to roll. It rolled over a few times and blocked one of the cave entrances.

Hercules crept round to the other cave entrance. He put his bow and arrows on the ground with his knife and his club. If an arrow couldn't hurt the beast then his knife and club would be no use either.

He took a deep breath and walked into the cave. At first, he saw nothing. Then his eyes began to get used to the dark. He could just about see the shape of the rocks inside the cave. And there was something else. Two red lights.

"Strange," Hercules thought. Then he heard the breathing and he knew that they weren't lights – they were eyes!

The lion sprang at him with another terrible roar. Hercules just had time to jump up onto a rock. The lion turned and sprang at him again, its red eyes flashing. Hercules jumped out of the way as the lion's great claws slashed at his legs. Then before the lion could attack again, Hercules jumped onto its back and put his huge arms around its neck.

The lion hissed and spat and roared.

It crashed against the cave walls trying to knock Hercules off its back.

But Hercules hung on, slowly squeezing the air out of the lion's lungs. Just as Hercules thought he had no strength left, the lion gave a final hiss and fell to the ground. It was dead.

***

A few days later, the king was in his palace, telling his friends about the stupid young man who said he was going to be famous forever.

"He will be famous for a day when he gets eaten by the lion," said the king. "Then he will be forgotten."

Just then, there was a loud knock at the door.

"Who is there?" said the king.

Hercules walked in. The king could not believe his eyes. Hercules was wearing the lion's mane like a hoodie.

"I am the great Hercules," he said. "I am going to be famous forever. I have proved it!"

The Sky Trick

The king was very cross that Hercules had killed the lion. He didn't want Hercules to be a hero. So he made a list of impossible tasks he thought Hercules would not be able to do.

The king hoped Hercules would be killed doing the tasks. But Hercules was so big and so strong he could do every task. On the king's list of tasks were capturing magical creatures and killing terrible monsters. But Hercules could do them all. After ten tasks, the king was running out of ideas.

"For your next task," said the king, "you are to bring me the golden apples of the Hesperides."

"What are they?" asked Hercules.

“That’s for you to find out,” said the king. “Off you go.”

Hercules picked up his club and set off. He asked everyone he met about the golden apples, but most people just shook their heads. Some people remembered stories about golden apples that their parents had told them when they were children. But nobody was sure the apples were real.

Hercules went for a swim in the river to think about what to do next. He thought the king had sent him off to find something that wasn't real.

"If I do find the golden apples of the Hesperides," thought Hercules, "I'd like to throw one at him!"

Hercules did not know it, but he was being watched by a tree spirit.

"I can help you find the Hesperides," she said.

Hercules looked around but he couldn't see anyone.

"You can't see me," laughed the spirit. "But I can see you. If you want to find the golden apples of the Hesperides, you must speak to the Old Man of the Sea."

"Who's he?" asked Hercules. But the spirit had gone.

Hercules was cross. First the king sent him to look for some apples he had never heard of. Then a spirit he couldn't see told him to go and find a man he had never heard of.

"Well, the sea must be a good place to look for the Old Man of the Sea," thought Hercules. So he set off.

For days and days Hercules walked by the sea. Everyone he met had heard of the Old Man of the Sea. But nobody knew where he was. Hercules was getting really fed up.

One morning he was walking along a beach. He stepped over a huge pile of seaweed. He stopped and looked at it. Could the seaweed be moving?

Hercules looked closer. Yes! The seaweed was moving very gently up and down. It was almost as if it were breathing!

Hercules pulled away some of the seaweed and saw an old, wrinkly foot.

"This must be the Old Man of the Sea!" Hercules thought. He grabbed the foot. The Old Man woke up. Hercules saw his angry green eyes. He had long, curly white hair and a very long red and yellow beard.

The Old Man said some words that Hercules didn't understand. The sound of the waves grew louder and louder.

Suddenly the man disappeared. In his place was a huge fish.

Hercules gripped the fish's slippery tail with both hands. It flapped around, lifting Hercules off his feet and waving him around in the air.

Hercules saw the fish's angry green eyes change to blue. And then the fish disappeared. In its place was a large dolphin.

The dolphin's blue eyes stared at Hercules as he clung on to its tail. It tried to fling Hercules away.

But Hercules held on until he saw the dolphin's blue eyes turn red. Then the dolphin disappeared. In its place was a giant crab, as big as a rowing boat.

Hercules grabbed the back of the crab's shell. The crab's claws stabbed at the air, trying to get at Hercules.

It ran from side to side, trying to throw Hercules off its back. But Hercules did not let go. Then the crab disappeared.

Hercules was holding the Old Man's foot again.

"OK," said the old man. "You win. What is it you want?"

Hercules told the Old Man of the Sea about the task the king had set for him.

"I know all about the golden apples of the Hesperides," said the old man.

"They belonged to Zeus, king of the gods. They grew in a magic garden in North Africa. The garden was looked after by three tree spirits called the Hesperides. It was guarded by a dragon with one hundred heads.

“Not even you are strong enough to kill that dragon,” said the Old Man of the Sea. “You must find Atlas, the giant god. The tree spirits are his daughters. Maybe he could get the apples for you.”

Hercules thanked the old man and set off to find the giant god called Atlas. Hercules knew what had happened to Atlas and he didn’t think it was going to be easy to get him to help find the golden apples.

Hercules had been told that, long ago, Atlas had attacked Zeus, king of the gods. Atlas lost the fight. Zeus punished him by making him hold the sky on his back for all time.

Hercules knew that the only way Atlas could go and get the apples was if somebody else held the sky for him. Hercules was very strong, but he was not stupid enough to think he could do the job of a giant god without help.

When Hercules got to the mountain where Atlas lived, he still did not know what to do. He lit a fire and lay down to sleep. In his dreams, he prayed to the goddess who had told him to choose between an easy life and a hard life that would be remembered forever.

As he dreamed and prayed, the shape of his goddess appeared in the fire.

"How are you enjoying your famous life?" the goddess asked.

"It's good to be famous," said Hercules. "And I've done every impossible task the king has set me. But this one is too much."

“I’ll help you,” said the goddess. She stared at some rocks. Hercules watched as a tunnel opened up in front of him. The goddess said, “You will find Atlas through that tunnel. Tomorrow, when you wake up, you will have the strength of a god. You will be strong enough to hold the sky for one day. After that, if you are still holding the sky, it will crush you into dust.”

The goddess disappeared and Hercules fell asleep.

***

When Hercules woke up his body felt different. He kicked a rock onto the fire. But instead of rolling onto the fire, the rock flew off the side of the mountain and kept going for miles and miles until it crashed into another mountain.

Hercules remembered what the goddess in his dream had said. He really did have the strength of a god. He had no time to lose. The tunnel from his dream was still there, and Hercules ran through it and out the other side.

There in front of him was Atlas. He was carved out of rock. His huge stone legs were bent. His huge back leaned forward. And on his back he held the sky.

"Atlas!" Hercules called. "The goddess sent me here to help you."

"I can't turn my head," said the giant god. "Come round to where I can see you."

So Hercules walked around until he was staring up into the giant god's face.

"She told me to give you a rest for a day," Hercules said. "All you have to do is go and get the golden apples of the Hesperides. If you promise to do that then I will hold the sky for you for a day."

"Well," said Atlas. "I could do with a rest. If all I have to do is get the apples, then we have a deal. Put your club down and I'll pass you the sky."

So Hercules bent his legs and his back like Atlas. Then he reached up and took the weight of the sky on his back.

Atlas moved away.

"Oh, that's better," he said. He stood up tall and rubbed his shoulders. Then he turned and walked away towards the sun.

***

When Atlas came back, he was carrying the branch of an apple tree. The golden apples hung down and shone in the sunlight.

"Here are your apples," said Atlas. "And now I must go." The giant began to walk away.

"Wait!" shouted Hercules. "We had a deal! This was just for a day!"

The giant god laughed. "We agreed I would bring you the apples. I never promised to carry the sky again."

Hercules thought of the goddess and her warning. His strength would only last for one day.

"You're right," Hercules said. "You've been holding the heavens for years. It's my turn now. But before you leave, I need your help for a moment."

"What do you need?" Atlas asked.

"It's my back," said Hercules. "If I'm going to hold up the sky forever I just need to move a bit. I just need to get myself into the right position. If you could just hold the sky for a moment while I move?"

"Oh, all right," said Atlas and he slowly lifted the sky off Hercules and put it on his own back.

"Thank you!" shouted Hercules, grabbing his club. "And thank you for the apples." Then he ran off back through the tunnel.

Atlas gave a giant roar of anger. But Hercules was free. He had his apples and he had proved that he could do the impossible. Again. He set off back to the king's palace.

He knocked at the palace door.

"Who is there?" said the king.

Hercules walked in. The king could not believe his eyes. Hercules was holding the golden apples.

"I am the great Hercules," he said. "I am going to be famous forever. I have proved it!"

The Hound of Hell

The king set Hercules one last task.

"You must find hell," said the king.

"What?" said Hercules.

"Then you must go down into hell," said the king.

"You must be joking!" said Hercules.

"And you must bring back Cerberus," said the king.

"Oh no!" said Hercules. "That's impossible!"

Cerberus was the monster dog who guarded hell. Its job was to stop the dead people from getting out.

"But no living person has ever gone down to hell before!" said Hercules.

"Not my problem," the king said. "You said you wanted to be famous forever. Then I order you to bring me Cerberus. Off you go!"

"This one really is impossible!" Hercules thought. "Nobody even knows where hell is!"

Hercules needed help. He needed somebody who knew all about hell and death and the gods. So, he went to the temple to find a priest. On the way he thought about Cerberus. Everyone knew the dog had been born in hell itself. It was the size of a horse. It had three heads and it had a snake for a tail. This task was not going to be easy.

At the temple the priest told Hercules how the dead get to hell.

"When you die," said the priest, "your spirit goes to the banks of the river Stix. Then Charon, the boatman, rows you across the river. But you have to pay him and you have to be dead. That's why we put a coin in the mouth of a dead body when we bury it, so the dead person can pay Charon. Then when you get to the other side of the river you will see a cave. That is the entrance to hell. Cerberus lives just inside the cave. He stops anyone trying to get back out of hell."

Hercules thought for a bit. Then he said, "Maybe this isn't such an impossible task. I don't need Charon to take me across the river. I can swim!"

"Wrong," the priest said. "The water of the river Stix is black and full of poison. If you swim in it, you will die. You will have to make Charon take you across. And he has never taken a living person across before."

Hercules thought a bit more.

"But if Cerberus lives at the entrance to hell then I don't have to go down into hell at all!"

"Wrong again," said the priest. "Hades is the god king of hell. If you take his guard dog without asking him first, he will find you and kill you and burn your soul forever!"

***

It was midnight when Hercules got to the river Stix. He put a gold coin in his mouth and lay down on the ground. He pretended to be dead. Soon he heard a boat coming towards him.

An old, old voice called out, “Who is waiting to cross the Stix and enter hell? And do you have a coin for me?”

Hercules waited until the boat was right by the riverbank. Then he jumped up and grabbed the boat. Charon was wearing a black cloak with a hood over his head. His skin was grey. He looked like death itself.

"You're not dead!" said Charon.

"But I need to cross the river," said Hercules. "And you're going to take me, or I'll never let go of this boat!"

Charon looked at Hercules. He saw Hercules had huge muscles. He saw the lion skin on his back. Charon knew he could not win a fight with this hulk.

"OK," he said, "I will take you across."

Hercules got into the boat and gave Charon the gold coin. Charon began to row the boat across the river.

At last they got to the other side.

"Thank you," said Hercules. "See you later."

"No, you won't," said Charon. "No one comes back from hell."

Hercules found the cave that the priest had told him about. He stood at the entrance and looked around, but there was no sign of Cerberus.

Hercules walked into the cave.

The cave went down, deep underground. After walking for a bit, Hercules came to a huge cavern. It was so big that Hercules couldn't see the roof, or the walls on the other side. But he could hear cries of pain.

"This does not sound good," thought Hercules.

The cavern was full of the spirits of the dead. He saw a man pushing a huge round rock up a slope. When the man was nearly at the top, the rock rolled back down the slope. The man followed the rock down and began rolling it up again.

"What are you doing?" Hercules asked.

"I was a murderer. This is my punishment," the man said. "I must push this rock forever."

Hercules saw another man standing in a pool of water up to his neck. The man's tongue was sticking out. His lips were cracked and dry. But when he bent his head to drink from the pool, the water level went down. It was always just out of reach.

"What did you do wrong?" Hercules asked. But the man's throat was so dry he could not speak.

Next, Hercules saw some women. They were trying to move water from one pool to another. They all carried water buckets.

But the buckets had holes in the bottom and so they were empty by the time the women got to the other pool.

"We killed our husbands," said one of the women. "This is our punishment. All day and all night forever, we fill our buckets, but we can never move any water to the other pool."

"Where will I find Hades?" Hercules asked.

"In the next cavern," said one of the women.

The second cavern was very bright. The walls sparkled with millions of glittering jewels. Hades and his queen sat on huge stone thrones in the middle of the cavern.

Hades looked strong and healthy and happy. The queen looked weak and pale and sad.

"Welcome, Hercules," said Hades. "No other living person has been brave enough, or mad enough, to enter my kingdom. Why are you here?"

"Great Hades," said Hercules, "I came here to ask if I can borrow Cerberus."

Hades laughed. "Why do you want to take Cerberus to the land of the living?"

"My goddess told me I would be famous forever," Hercules said. "But I have to do every task my king set me. My king told me to bring Cerberus to him."

"Then your king wants you to die," said Hades. "He has set you an impossible task. But you have done well to get this far. If you can catch Cerberus, without hurting him, then you may take him to your king for a day."

Hercules was amazed.

"Thanks!" he said. "I thought you would say no. I thought I was going to die when I came here!"

"You still might," said Hades. "You still might."

Hercules set off back through the caverns and out of hell. When he could see the night sky ahead, he knew he was near the entrance to the cave. He stopped and listened. He heard loud snoring. Cerberus must be sleeping nearby.

Hercules put his club on the ground. He pulled his lion's mane hood over his head. He pulled the lion's skin around his neck. Very slowly, he crept forwards.

Hercules could hear Cerberus snoring, but still he couldn't see him. Then his foot kicked a small stone. It rolled along the rocky ground. At once, the sound of snoring stopped. There were a few seconds of silence. Then Hercules heard three very loud growls.

Hercules began to shake with fear. He looked up and saw six red eyes looking down at him. Hercules saw the sharp fangs. He saw the snake tail waving around on the dog's back.

Then Cerberus growled again and attacked.

Hercules jumped back just in time. But his heel hit a rock and he fell to the ground. Cerberus jumped onto Hercules. The dog bent down to sink its fangs into Hercules. One of the dog's heads went for Hercules' head. One of the dog's heads went for Hercules' chest. The third head went for Hercules' throat. But when Cerberus tried to snap his jaws shut, they could not get through the lion's skin.

The snake tail hissed and spat. But before it could attack, Hercules grabbed it and bashed its head on a rock.

Cerberus rolled off Hercules. He was shocked that his sharp fangs could not bite Hercules. Hercules jumped to his feet. He pulled the lion's skin off his back and held it up in one hand.

Cerberus attacked Hercules again. Hercules stepped to one side and wrapped the lion's skin around the monster dog's chest. Then he jumped

onto Cerberus and slid the lion's skin up around the dog's three necks. He had the three heads in a single noose!

Hercules squeezed and squeezed. Cerberus tried to shake off the lion's skin. But he was getting weaker and weaker. Then he fainted and fell to the ground.

***

When Hercules got back to the king's palace, he was carrying Cerberus on his back. The king could not believe his eyes.

"I thought you would be dead by now," said the king.

"I've done what you asked," said Hercules and he dropped Cerberus at the king's feet.

When Cerberus hit the floor, he began to wake up. The king turned white with fear.

"Get it away from me!" he screamed.

Hercules put his lion's skin around Cerberus again. But he didn't hold the skin too tight. Slowly, Cerberus got to his feet.

"Please! Please!" cried the king. "I have no more tasks for you. You've done the impossible.

You are the greatest hero who ever lived. And I never want to see you again. Just please make it go away!"

So, Hercules took Cerberus back to Hades.

And was Hercules famous forever? Well, we are still telling his story now...

Bonus Bits!

Greek Mythology

There are a number of Greek myths that we still read and study today.

Myths are stories which were told in ancient times and were passed from person to person. They usually include a hero or heroine facing tasks or something evil. Sometimes they have a moral or a message. They also often include fantastical creatures.

Quiz Time

See how good your knowledge of the story is by answering these multiple-choice questions. Look back at the story for help if you need to.

1. What did Hercules want to be?

a. Happy

b. Famous

c. Tired

2. What part of the lion did the king want Hercules to bring him?

a. the skin

b. the claw

c. the mane

3. Who does the spirit tell Hercules he must speak to?

   a. the Old Man of the Sea

   b. the Old Woman of the Woods

   c. the Old Man of the Earth

4. Who got the apples for Hercules?

   a. the goddess

   b. Atlas

   c. the spirits

5. What does Cerberus have for a tail?

   a. a lightning bolt

   b. a snake

   c. a spear

Pill 02-05-21

What do you Think?

- Do you think Hercules became famous forever? Why?
- Which of the three tasks described in detail in the text do you think was the most difficult?
- How do you think Hercules felt when he thought he would be left holding the sky forever?

ANSWERS TO QUIZ TIME

1b, 2a, 3a, 4b, 5b

PILLGWENLLY